P9-CLH-049

Sir Charlie Stinky Socks
and the Really BIG Adventure

Kristina
Stephenson

EGMONT
USA
NEW YORK

Once up·on a time,
there was a **deep, dark forest**,
where monstrous trees groaned,
terrible beasties moaned,
and wiggly woos waited
to tickle your toes.

In the middle of the forest,
surrounded by thorny bushes,
there stood a tall, tall tower
with a pointy roof.
At the bottom of the tower
was a big wooden door.

Inside the tower
a windy, windy staircase
didn't stop winding
until it reached
a little wooden door,
right at the very top.

And what was behind
that little wooden door?
Well, nobody knew,
because nobody ever went there.

THE END.

At least . . . not until the day when . . .

. . . a bold, brave knight,
Sir Charlie Stinky Socks,
and his faithful, fearless cat, Envelope,
decided that the time had come for
a really big adventure.

Sir Charlie picked his best sword,
packed some sandwiches,
a big bottle of water, and
a favorite little something
for the journey (just in case).

And with a song in his heart
he mounted his good gray mare.

Clip clop,
Clip clop,
Clippety clippety clop!

Over the hills
and far away rode Sir Charlie and his cat.

(Oh, and a wily witch with a watch followed behind on a broom.)

At last they came
to a **deep, dark forest**,
where monstrous trees *groaned*
and **terrible beasties** *moaned*.

Envelope *shivered*.

The good gray mare *quivered*.

(While the witch with
the watch covered her eyes.)

But brave Sir Charlie
stood steady in his boots.

"Sssshhhhhh!" he whispered into the woods.
"'Tis I . . . Sir Charlie Stinky Socks
with a song to *soothe* you."

And as Sir Charlie sang his lullaby
the trees stopped groaning.

But the **terrible beasties**
went on moaning.

"Stop your moaning," cried the knight.
"Come out and eat me if you dare!"

Out of the darkness
crept
six
slobbering
beasties.

That fearless cat, Envelope, scampered away!

The good gray mare fled!

(And even the wily witch
with the watch
trembled behind a tree.)

But bold Sir Charlie did not turn.
Brave Sir Charlie did not run.

Instead he drew his trusty
sword and did what any
good knight would do . . .

. . . he smiled and cut up his sandwiches!

The **beasties** stood and stared.
They were hairy, hideous creatures
indeed, but they were **more** scared
of Sir Charlie Stinky Socks than
he was of them!

Charlie fed the beasties
and the beasties
stopped moaning.

(And the wily witch
with the watch
looked on with a grin
and checked the time.)

But this was no way to end
a really big adventure.

So Sir Charlie Stinky Socks rescued his cat, rallied his good gray mare,
and set off once again, never minding the wiggly woos who waited in the grass or
the six not so terrible beasties who followed him.

The forest grew **thicker** and the bushes became thorny.
Lucky for Envelope and the good gray mare
that Sir Charlie Stinky Socks led the way
with his trusty sword.

Wooshity thwack, wooshity thwack, choppity choppity chop!

It was thirsty work for a bold, brave knight;
how glad he was to have a big bottle of water by his side.

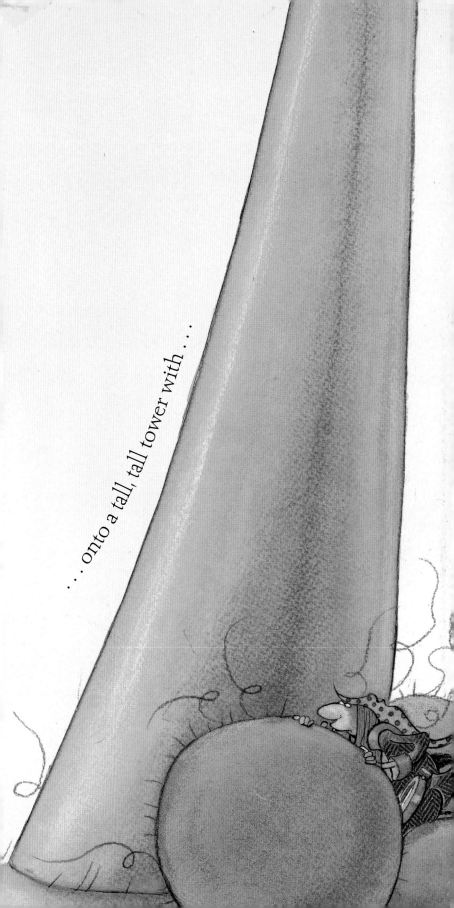

. . . onto a tall, tall tower with . . .

. . . a pointy roof.

And then, at last, they came to
a clearing in the trees
where the sun threw down
its pale yellow light . . .

But it
also threw
its light onto . . .

. . . a long, green dragon!
He was *frightful* and *fearsome*
and coughing out *fire*
while he stomped
in a temper around
the tower.

Ha-ha!
thought Sir Charlie Stinky Socks.
Just the thing for a really big adventure!

"Stop your roaring, dragon!"
he commanded.

But the dragon did *not* stop.
He went on *coughing* out fire.
He went on *belching* out smoke.
And now his eyes were fixed firmly
on Sir Charlie Stinky Socks.

Was this the end of the line for the bold, brave knight?

Oh my!

Envelope didn't hang around to find out.
And neither did the good gray mare.

Only a worried, wily witch and a couple of wiggly woos watched.

But bold Sir Charlie
did not flinch.

Brave Sir Charlie
did not flicker.

He took out his big bottle
of water and . . .

. . . kind, clever
Sir Charlie Stinky Socks
gave that old dragon
a long,
cooooooool
drink.

Aaaaaaahhhhh!

"Now that you've stopped coughing,"
said the knight to the long, green dragon,
"tell me what's at the top of this tower."

The dragon looked up.
The dragon looked at Sir Charlie.
The dragon scratched
his scaly head and said,
"My dear old thing, I haven't a clue.
It's not a dragon's place to ask,
you know – just . . . to do."

"Then why don't we find out?"
said Sir Charlie with a grin.

The wily witch took one last look at her watch, jumped for joy, and flew off on her broom as Charlie pushed open the big wooden door.

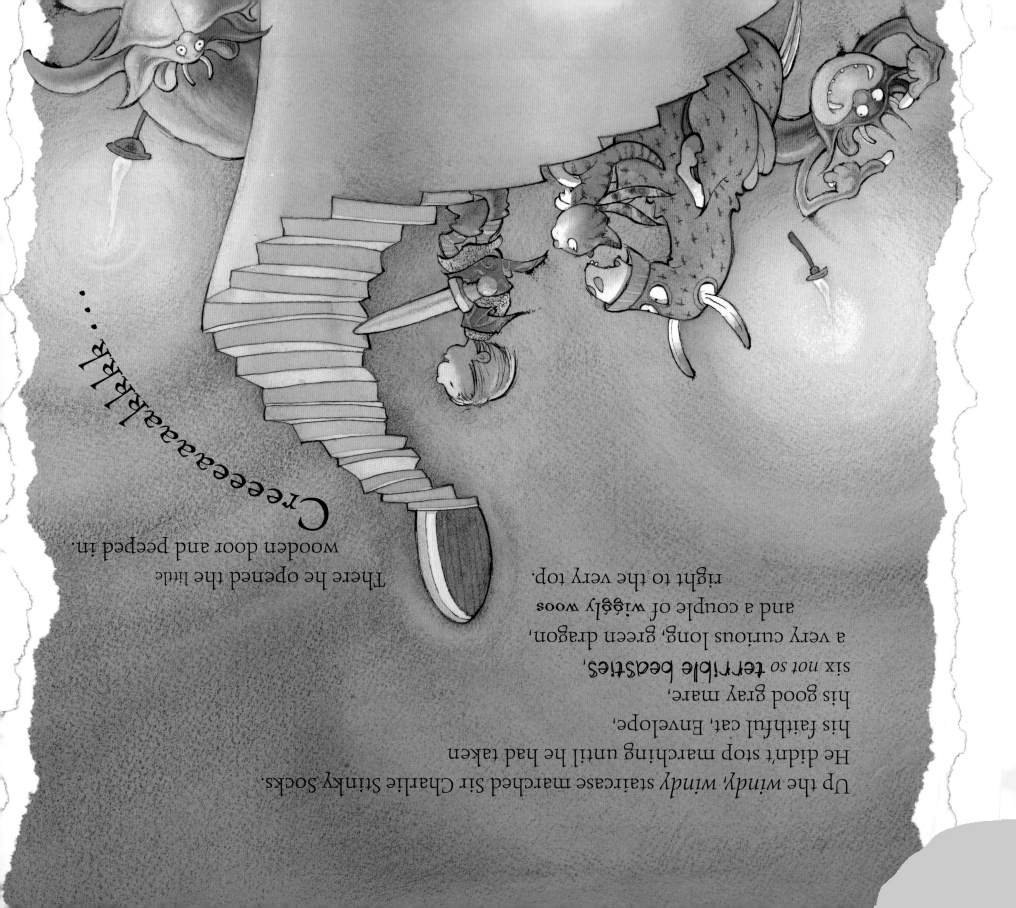

Creeeeaaaakkk . . .

There he opened the little
wooden door and peeped in.

Up the *windy, windy* staircase marched Sir Charlie Stinky Socks.
He didn't stop marching until he had taken
his faithful cat, Envelope,
his good gray mare,
six *not so* **terrible beasties**,
a very curious long, green dragon,
and a couple of wiggly woos
right to the very top.

A big black cauldron stood in
the middle of the room, and stirring
it was the wily witch (of course).

By her side sat a little princess,
weeping and *wailing*
in a pool of tears.

Sir Charlie looked at the princess.

Sir Charlie looked at the bubbling pot.

Sir Charlie didn't wait another minute.
He drew his trusty sword,
and bounded over to rescue
                    the little princess.

"Stop your weeping!" cried the knight.
**"Sir Charlie Stinky Socks is here
to save you from the pot."**

The witch cackled.

"I'm not going to cook the *princess*!" squealed the witch.
"I'm cooking the food for her birthday party.
It's today, at three, you see. I do it every year,
you know. I blow up balloons
and decorate the tower.
I send out invitations –
hundreds of them!

And looky here!"
she cried, tip-tapping
at the face of
her watch.
"It's nearly three!
Yippee!"

"Then . . . why are you crying, princess?"
asked Sir Charlie.

That night the lights burned brightly
in the tall, tall tower with the pointy roof,
as a happy little princess
had a rip-roaring good time!

"Behold

Sir Charlie Stinky Socks and his friends!"

"Because," shrieked a *windy, windy* staircase surrounded by **thorns** dragon. And it's in **forest**, where wiggly your toes, hungry and monstrous so nobody ever comes!"

One, two,
three, four!

15

Over at the school yard,
when it's fine,
children all play, in a line.
How many children
can you count?

One, two, three, four!

Dad should go and take a peep. Perhaps Polly should try counting sheep?

One, two, three,
four, five ...

How many

balls can you count?

FUN FACTS

 Almost everyone in the world learns how to count by using their fingers.

 All kites used to have four sides. Now kites come in all sorts of shapes.

 The opposite sides of a die (or dice) added together always equal seven.

 Most boat owners name their boats.

 In 24 hours, Ashrita Furman of New York City jumped rope 130,000 times.

WORDS TO KNOW

beach—a sandy area next to a body of water such as a lake or an ocean

breeze—wind that blows gently

dice—small, marked cubes with dots ranging from one to six on each side

kites—light frames covered with cloth or paper that can be flown in the air

pavement—a hard covering, usually made from cement, for a sidewalk, path, parking lot, or other area

school yard—an area outside a school building that is used for playing and exercising

TO LEARN MORE

At the Library

McGrath, Barbara Barbieri. *The Cheerios Counting Book.* New York: Scholastic, 1998.

Ryan, Pam Muñoz, and Jerry Pallotta. *The Crayon Counting Book.* Watertown, Mass.: Charlesbridge, 1996.

Voce, Louise. *Over In the Meadow: A Traditional Counting Rhyme.* Cambridge, Mass.: Candlewickpress, 1994.

On the Web

FactHound offers a safe, fun way to find Web sites related to this book.

All of the sites on FactHound have been researched by our staff.

1. Visit *www.facthound.com*

2. Type in this special code: 1404810625

3. Click on the FETCH IT button.

Your trusty FactHound will fetch the best Web sites for you!

INDEX

Look for all of the books in the All Sorts of Things series:

All Sorts of Clothes

All Sorts of Noises

All Sorts of Numbers

All Sorts of Shapes